Showdown at the Okeydokey Corral

by Cathy Hapka

Disney PRESS

New York

Library of Congress Catalog Card Number: 00-101750

ISBN 0-7868-4442-6

For more Disney Press fun, visit www.disneybooks.com

Contents

1. Hats Off to Woody!

"**W**hoa!" Jessie the cowgirl was walking across the Okeydokey Corral when a desert whirlwind suddenly swept around her, almost knocking her off her feet. She grabbed for her hat, but it was too late. The twister lifted it right off her head. "Hey! Give that back!"

The wind tossed Jessie's hat high into the air, then spun it across the corral. Jessie raced after it. But the twister was too fast. Every time Jessie thought she might be able to grab her hat, the twister dipped, swirled, and swooped, keeping the hat just out of reach.

The twister spun toward the corral gate. "Come back here, hat thief," Jessie cried, leaping forward once again to grab at her hat. But once again she missed. The twister turned and spun right through the gate, heading out into the desert. For a moment Jessie thought it was going to spin off into the horizon with her hat.

Instead, the wind spun faster and faster—until the hat flew right out of the top of the whirlwind. It tumbled through the air and landed high atop a prickly cactus!

"Oh, my," Jessie said, staring up at the cactus as the twister spun off. The cactus was almost as tall as the town's water tower. "How am I going to get my hat back?"

She remembered the lasso hanging from her belt. Maybe she could rope the hat and pull it down.

"Okay, cactus," she said as she looped her rope carefully and took aim. "I've been practicing. Just this morning I roped the new calf three times in a row! He even woke up before the third time. Now hold still."

She let the rope fly. But instead of lassoing the hat, it looped around one of the cactus's prickly arms.

"Doggone it!" Jessie exclaimed, yanking at her rope. It took a few tries to pull the rope loose from the cactus's spiky thorns, but she finally got it back.

She tried again to rope the hat. The same thing happened. She tossed the lasso once more. Once more, it landed squarely around the cactus arm.

"Rotten rattlesnakes!" she cried in frustration.

"I may be the rip-roaringest roper in the Wild West, but I'll never be able to lasso my hat with those long, thorny cactus arms in the way."

She sat down to rest, staring up at her hat. It looked so lonely way up there atop the tall cactus. How in the world was she going to get it back?

I can't rope it, she thought, ticking the possibilities off on her fingers. I can't climb the cactus to get it. I don't want to cut down the cactus.

While she was thinking, Sheriff Woody came loping toward her across the corral, holding a bag of fresh roasted peanuts. "Howdy, Jessie," he called, tossing a handful of peanuts into his mouth. "What are you doing out here by the corral?"

Jessie told him the whole story. "I guess I could wait for the wind to blow my hat down again," she said at the end. "It might take a while, though. And that's my best hat!"

"Don't worry," Woody said, crunching on a peanut. "I'll figure out a way to get your hat."

"Like what? I already tried roping it," Jessie

said with a sigh. "Maybe I should just go down to the general store and buy a new hat."

"No, don't do that yet." Woody was staring thoughtfully up at the stranded hat, stroking his chin. "I have an idea."

He grabbed a handful of peanuts. Taking aim, he tossed them as hard as he could, straight up at Jessie's hat. A few of them bounced off of the cactus, but the rest landed on the hat's wide brim.

"What are you doing?" Jessie asked hopefully. "It doesn't seem likely you'll be able to knock it loose with a few peanuts."

"That's not what I'm doing," Woody said with a smile. "Just watch."

Jessie looked up, wondering if the hot desert sun was making Woody light-headed. How was a handful of peanuts going to get her hat back?

She saw a black speck on the horizon. Then another. They came closer, until Jessie could see that they were crows.

"Caw! Caw!" cried the crows, swooping toward the cactus. They swept down and grabbed for the peanuts. As they grabbed the peanuts in their claws, they dislodged the hat

from the thorny cactus. The hat tumbled down and landed on the ground at Jessie's feet.

"One hat, ma'am," Woody said with a grin. "As ordered."

Jessie laughed with delight. "Thanks!" she exclaimed, putting her hat back on. "I never would've thought to try that!"

"That's why I'm the sheriff," Woody said modestly, tipping his own hat. "It's my job to take care of other people when they can't take care of themselves."

"What do you mean?" Jessie said. "I can *always* take care of myself."

"No offense, Jessie," Woody said. "I just meant

that there often comes a time when an ordinary cowpoke needs a little extra help. That's when I step in."

"An *ordinary* cowpoke?" Jessie exclaimed. "I'm not ordinary!"

Woody shrugged. "There's nothing wrong with being ordinary," he said. "We can't all be sheriff—that's all I'm saying."

"Oh, yeah?" Jessie said. "I don't have to be sheriff to be a better cowpoke than you! I can out-cowpoke you any day of the week!"

2. The Prospector's Stinky Solution

Woody held up his hands. "I didn't mean it that way," he protested. "We're a team, Jessie. Have a peanut." He held out his bag of peanuts.

"No, thanks." Jessie frowned. At first she had thought that Woody was just joking around. But now she was starting to think that Sheriff Woody really needed to be taken down a peg. Did he actually honest-to-goodness think he was a better cowpoke than she was? Well, Jessie would teach him a lesson he wouldn't soon forget. "So how about it? Want to see which of us is the better cowpoke?" she said.

Woody laughed nervously. He wasn't sure why Jessie was getting upset. "Who cares who's the better cowpoke?" he said. "You're a good cowpoke, I'm a good cowpoke. Come on, let's just forget it and go check on the new calf."

"What's the matter, Sheriff?" Jessie crossed her arms over her chest with a sly smile. "Are you chicken?"

"No way!" Woody said. "I just think it's silly."

"Bok bok bok!" Jessie cackled, grinning and flapping her arms like wings.

Woody sighed and rolled his eyes. "Quit it, Jessie."

"Quit what? Quit calling you a belly-button-pickin', lily-livered chicken?"

"That's right," Woody replied. Jessie's teasing was starting to make him feel a little hot under the collar. "And while you're at it, you can quit saying you're a better cowpoke than I am. After all, you couldn't even rope your own hat off of a cactus plant."

Jessie felt her face turn red. How dare he bring that up? He knew the cactus's arms had been in the way! She tossed her head. "I'll never

stop saying it," she cried. "Because I happen to be *twice* the cowpoke you'll ever be!"

Woody couldn't let that pass. He knew that Jessie was a great cowpoke, but that didn't mean he was about to admit that she was better than him. "No way," he said. "Everybody in the West knows that I'm *three* times the cowpoke *you'll* ever be."

"You've been out in the hot sun too long," Jessie declared, "because it's as plain as the spots on your vest that I'm *four* times finer a cowpoke on my worst day than you are on your best."

"What in the hee-haw is all the shouting about?" Woody turned and saw the Prospector hurrying toward them with Bullseye the horse at his side.

"It's nothing," Woody said. "Jessie and I were just having, er, a discussion."

"Yeah," Jessie exclaimed. "A discussion about how our sheriff is a lily-livered, egg-laying, over-cooked *chicken*!"

"A chicken, eh?" the Prospector said. "That true, Sheriff Woody?"

"Of course not," Woody exclaimed, trying to hold on to his temper. Enough was enough. He was tired of the whole argument. He knew that Jessie didn't really think he was a chicken, just like he knew that the only reason she couldn't lasso her own hat was because the cactus's arms had been in the way. Things had gone far enough, and it was up to him to stop them. He just wanted the two of them to be friends again. "Okay, listen here, Jessie," he said, turning back

to face her with his hands on his hips. "What do you want me to say? That you're just as good a cowpoke as I am?"

Jessie grinned. Now they were getting somewhere. She knew that Woody knew she was a fine cowpoke, just like he was. All she wanted was to hear him admit it. "Well, I guess that would be—"

"Hold it there," the Prospector interrupted, scratching his beard. There was a mischievous glint in his eyes. "Doesn't sound like she was asking for an apology to me, Sheriff. Seems more like she was issuing a challenge. And a *real* cowpoke never backs down from a challenge, isn't that right?"

Woody gulped. "He—he doesn't?"

"Nope." The Prospector turned to Jessie. "A real cowpoke stands up for what he or she believes in, no matter what the consequences. Wouldn't you agree, Jessie?"

"She does?" Jessie said. Then she added, "Um, but that's okay. As long as Woody admits we're both good cowpokes, I could probably let it go."

"Oh, he may admit it," the Prospector said,

shaking a finger under her nose. "But does he *mean* it?"

Jessie blinked. "Um . . ."

"Nope!" the Prospector cried. "You can't go by what he *says*. You have to go by what he really *thinks*. And what he *thinks* is that he's the king of the cowpokes!"

"Now, wait a minute. . ." Woody protested.

But the Prospector wasn't listening. He was rubbing his hands together happily. "Nope, there's only one way to find out the truth!" he exclaimed. "A cowpoke contest!"

3. Bullseye!

"**A** what?" Jessie asked.

"A who?" Woody added.

The Prospector nodded firmly and slapped his knee. "A cowpoke contest. How about it?"

Woody looked at Jessie. Jessie looked back at Woody.

"Come on!" the Prospector cried. "I thought you two were real cowpokes! And a real cowpoke never backs down, remember? So how about it? You aren't backing down, are ya?"

"Um, no sirree," Jessie said.

Woody cleared his throat. "Er, right," he agreed. "No sirree."

"Okay, then." The Prospector smiled. "Now, what can you do to prove which one of you is the

roughest, toughest cowpoke in the Wild West?"

Jessie shrugged. She wasn't sure what a cowpoke contest was supposed to be like. But she knew she wanted to win. If she didn't, the Prospector would probably tell everybody in town that Woody was a better cowpoke than she was.

She had to think of a good idea to prove that she was the better cowpoke. She glanced over and saw Bullseye scratching his shoulder on a fence post. That gave her an idea.

"You can't be a good cowpoke without being able to communicate with your horse," she said. "Why don't we see which of us is better with Bullseye?"

As soon as she said it, she wondered if it were a mistake. After all, Bullseye was Woody's horse.

"Yee-haw!" the Prospector exclaimed, clapping his hands. "A riding contest!"

"No, no, not riding," Jessie said, thinking fast. Woody rode Bullseye all the time. That wouldn't be fair. "I mean *real* communication. We'll see who can, er, teach Bullseye a better trick."

Woody blinked in surprise. Teach Bullseye a

trick? He wasn't sure about that. Bullseye was a good horse, but he didn't know any tricks as far as Woody knew.

Still, he couldn't back down now, or Jessie would tell everyone he was a belly-button-pickin' chicken. "You're on," he agreed. "Go ahead, Jessie. You can go first."

"Okeydokey. Here I go." Taking a deep breath, Jessie walked over to Bullseye. What kind of trick could she teach him? She tried to remember the tricks she'd seen her neighbor's old hound dog do. "Sit, Bullseye!" she said. "Sit!" She tapped the horse on the rump. "Come on, boy. Sit!"

Bullseye gave her a strange look and a confused snort. He stood where he was, swishing his tail.

Jessie patted Bullseye on the rear again. "Sit, boy!" she said desperately. "C'mon, please?"

"That's enough," Woody declared, stepping forward and trying to sound confident. "Now step back, little lady, and see how a real cowpoke trains his horse."

He cleared his throat. He had no idea if Bullseye could do any tricks. But he was going to

give it his best cowpoke try.

"Okay, Bullseye," Woody said, tapping the horse on the knee. "Put 'er there, pardner. Shake." He stuck out his hand.

Bullseye stepped forward and nudged Woody's hand with his nose. He snorted, looking for a treat.

"Now come on, Bullseye," Woody pleaded, taking a step backward and holding out his hand again. "Shake! Shake!"

Bullseye cocked his head thoughtfully. He blinked. He started to lift one front hoof off the ground. . . .

Suddenly a great, big, nasty horsefly roared in from the desert. It zoomed through the corral, buzzing in all directions, whirling and twirling in everyone's faces. Bullseye took one look at the horsefly and chased it in the other direction. Bullseye and the noisy horsefly disappeared over the horizon.

"Too bad, Sheriff," Jessie said with a smirk. "Looks like your horse is a no-trick pony."

Woody frowned. If only that twister of a horsefly hadn't shown up at the wrong moment,

he would have won. But he didn't want to be a bad sport and point that out. "Oh, well," he said instead. "I guess we'll just have to call it a draw."

"A draw?" Jessie thought about that for a second. "Well, okay, I guess that would be—"

"That wasn't a *draw*," the Prospector insisted. "That was nothin' but a dad-burn *joke*." He waved one hand after Bullseye. "That silly horse ruined everything. No, if we really want to see who really has a way with animals, it should be with an animal like Ol' Diablo there." He turned to point at a large bull chewing its cud in the next corral. "I say, whichever one of you can ride that beastly bull around the corral is the roughest, toughest, all-time awesomest cowpoke this side of the Pecos!"

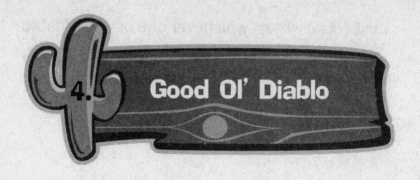

4. Good Ol' Diablo

Jessie blinked in surprise. Ol' Diablo was the fattest, laziest bull in the herd. "Ride him?" she said. "Why?"

"You're not chicken, are ya?" the Prospector asked mischievously.

"Of course not!" Jessie said immediately. Nobody called her a chicken! "Go ahead, Woody. It's your turn to go first."

"Okay." Woody thought the whole idea of riding Ol' Diablo was kind of silly. But he didn't want to say so. If he did, Jessie and the Prospector might think he was a feather-flappin' corn-peckin' chicken.

He walked over to Ol' Diablo and gave the bull a pat on the shoulder. Ol' Diablo hardly moved. He just turned his head slightly, still chewing his cud.

"Easy, big fella," Woody said soothingly. Ol' Diablo might be lazy, but he was still awfully large! Taking a deep breath, he hopped onto the bull's back. "Okay, Diablo," he said, kicking with his heels. "Giddy-up!"

The bull stood still for a moment. Then with a loud, weary sigh, Ol' Diablo buckled his knees and sank to the ground.

"Hey!" Woody hollered, his face turning as red as a desert sunset. "Get up, you lazy old bull!"

He waved his hat, bounced up and down, and kicked his heels. But Ol' Diablo just snorted lazily and rolled over onto his side, closing his big brown eyes. Woody jumped off his back just in time.

Jessie was buckled over laughing. "Pretty fancy bull riding there, Woody!" she called. "Are you going to do that at the next rodeo? It could be a whole new event—they can call it *bull dozing*!"

Woody scowled. He didn't like being laughed at, at least not when he wasn't trying to be funny. "I'd like to see you do better!" he told her hotly.

"No problem." Jessie swaggered toward Ol' Diablo, who was still lying on the ground snoring like a summer thunderstorm. "Get up, Diablo! We're going to show them how it's done. Yee-hah!"

She poked and prodded at the sleeping bull. She climbed up on his broad back and prodded him firmly with her heels.

30

Ol' Diablo stirred. "Git up!" Jessie yelled eagerly, certain that she was about to win the contest.

Ol' Diablo did stir. He sat straight up, and sent Jessie tumbling down the hill!

The drowsy bull yawned and stretched. Then he slumped back into a sound sleep.

This time it was Woody's turn to laugh. "Oh, yeah, that's a *lot* better," he said sarcastically.

"For a second there, I thought he might actually open both eyes."

Jessie scowled as she climbed to her feet and brushed the dust off her chaps. "Well, maybe I could've ridden him if you hadn't already put him to sleep."

"Oh yeah?" Woody stepped forward until the two of them were standing nose to nose. "Well, maybe we need to find a better way to prove that I'm the best cowpoke around."

"Maybe we do!" Jessie whirled to face the Prospector. "What do you think?" she asked him. "What else can we do to prove who's the roughest, toughest, all-time awesomest cowpoke in these parts?"

The Prospector shrugged. "Way I see it, if you can't get the bull to run, you two oughta do the running yourselves," he said. "How about a good old-fashioned footrace?"

5. The Really Big Race!

"**A** race?" Jessie scratched her head. "What does running a race have to do with being a cowpoke?"

"What's the matter?" Woody asked. He thought a footrace was a dumb idea, too. But he wasn't about to agree with Jessie. Not after the way she'd laughed at him. "You chicken?"

"Of course not." Jessie frowned. "I just think it's silly."

Woody winked at the Prospector. "She's chicken," he whispered. He wriggled one of his long, lanky legs. "I don't blame her, I suppose.

I'm awfully fast on my feet. A *good* cowpoke has to be quick, you know."

"Fine!" Jessie said, annoyed at the way Woody was acting. "If you want to race, let's race." She turned to the Prospector. "You can stand at the finish line and declare me the winner when I leave Sheriff Woody in my dust."

"All right, all right," the Prospector said with a chuckle. He hurried off across the corral.

"You can't win, you know," Woody said confidently. "You're the one who's going to be eatin'

dust." He hopped from foot to foot, warming up his legs.

"Oh, yeah?" Jessie bent over and touched her toes, stretching her muscles. "We'll just see about that."

About a hundred yards away, the Prospector drew a finish line in the sandy ground with the toe of his boot. Then he stepped back and shaded his eyes to check on the two cowpokes. "Ready to find out once and for all who's the roughest, toughest, all-time awesomest, gosh-darn greatest cowpoke in the Wild West?" he shouted.

Woody and Jessie lined up and got ready to run. "Ready!" they called.

"On your marks . . . get set . . ." The Prospector waved his hat in the air like a starter's flag. "Go!"

Jessie took off like a shot. She aimed straight for the finish line, her legs pumping. She would prove that she was every bit the cowpoke that Woody was if it was the last thing she did.

Beside her, Woody was just as determined as he sprinted forward. He couldn't let Jessie beat him. No sirree.

Slowly, Woody began to pull ahead of Jessie. First one step, then two . . . suddenly a rock appeared out of nowhere. Woody tripped on it, and he went flying.

"Aaaaaah!" he cried as he tumbled through the air and landed backside first on the dusty ground.

Jessie turned to see what had happened to Woody. When she saw him sitting on the ground, she grinned. Now there was no way he could beat her! "Yeee-hah!" she crowed.

As she turned back toward the finish line, Jessie was startled by a speedy jackrabbit hopping across her path! She leapt over it, but before she knew what was happening, she went flying face-first into the dirt.

"Ugh!" she exclaimed, spitting out a mouthful of sand. "I thing I bid my tongue!"

She stuck it out, trying to see. Meanwhile, Woody was pulling off his left boot. "I think my toe is broken," he moaned, waggling his foot inside its sock. "Does it look broken?"

Jessie looked. "I don't know," she said. "I thing I bid my tongue."

"No," Woody reported, peering at her tongue.

"Oh." Jessie touched it with her finger. "Well, it still hurts."

"So does my toe!" Woody complained. He wriggled his foot again. "Ow!"

The Prospector stared at them both in dismay. "Some rootin' tootin' cowpokes you two are," he exclaimed. "More like rootin' tootin' *crybabies* if you ask me! Can't even run a race without tripping over your own dad-blasted boots. I guess it's true, all cowpokes are good for anyway is spinnin' yarns and square-dancing."

"That's it!" Woody sat up straight and smiled, forgetting all about his toe. "That's how we can settle this. A dance contest!"

6. Dancin' Time!

"**U**m, okay," Jessie said weakly. "You're on."

What else could she say? If she backed out now, Woody would call her a fried chicken. And Jessie was no chicken—roasted or fried! But she *was* worried about beating Woody in a dance contest. The sheriff was so lean and lanky that everyone in town said he was looser than a long-necked goose.

"Oh well," Woody said, testing his toe. It was already feeling better. In fact, it was tapping in anticipation. "Let's get started!"

Jessie's stomach flip-flopped nervously as Woody quickly pulled his boot back on. She licked her lips with her tongue, which suddenly didn't seem to hurt quite so much. She searched her mind for a way out of the dancing idea. "Um, what about music?" she blurted. "We can't dance without music!"

"Hmm." Woody looked worried. "You could be right about that. Dancing just isn't the same without the tunes to back it up."

Jessie smiled, feeling relieved. "Oh, well," she said. "Too bad. I guess we'll just have to think of a different way to settle the contest."

"Don't be a dang fool. I'll just run on down to the saloon and borrow their Victrola record-playing machine," the Prospector said. "Wait here, and I'll be back in two shakes of a bronco's tail."

He hurried off toward town before either Jessie or Woody could answer. Jessie watched him go, her spirits sinking.

"Hope you don't mind if I warm up a little while we're waiting," Woody said. "I'm feeling kind of stiff after that fall just now."

He didn't look stiff. As Jessie watched, Woody did a cowboy jig right there in the corral. His feet flashed back and forth so fast that Jessie could hardly follow them. His arms wriggled and waggled over his head, and his chin nodded in time with his steps.

Finally Jessie couldn't watch anymore. Maybe Woody was a great dancer, but that didn't mean she was going to give up without a fight. If she did, she really would be a lily-livered, flabby-gizzard, belly-button-pickin', cacklin' chicken.

She would have to give dancing her best shot.

"I'm going to warm up, too," she announced.

Taking a deep breath, she started to dance. With no music to hold her back, she simply swung and swayed any way she wanted to. After a few seconds she forgot all about Woody. Dancing was fun! Before long she found herself hopping and spinning like an old pro.

"Wow," Woody said, stopping to stare. "You're a good dancer, Jessie."

Jessie was so surprised by the compliment that she stopped short as well. "Thanks," she said. "You're a good dancer, too."

"Thanks," Woody said. "Listen, Jessie. Maybe this whole contest thing is stupid. What do you say we—"

"Woody! Jessie!" The Prospector came running toward them at top speed, his face bright red and his breath coming in gasps. "Big trouble!"

"What is it, Prospector?" Woody asked. "What's wrong?"

The Prospector skidded to a stop. "It's the new calf!" he panted. "He just fell into the Rushing River!"

47

Jessie gasped. "Oh, no!" she cried. "We have to save the calf!"

"Let's go!" Woody turned and stuck two fingers in his mouth, whistling for Bullseye. A moment later he appeared at the edge of the corral.

"Come on, Bullseye!" Jessie cried. "To the river! We have a calf to save!"

Bullseye snorted and galloped toward them. He stopped short just long enough for Woody and Jessie to climb on his back, then whirled and raced off toward the river, leaving the Prospector

coughing in the cloud of dust from his hooves.

"Ride like the wind, Bullseye!" Woody shouted, holding on to Bullseye's mane. "Hurry!"

Jessie held on tight to Woody's belt. Both of them bounced up and down as Bullseye galloped over hill and dale, through cactus groves and tumbleweeds, past confused coyotes and blinking buzzards. Bullseye never slowed down, and the two riders never loosened their grip.

Finally, over the sound of the horse's hoofbeats, Woody and Jessie could hear another sound. It was the roaring, rumbling sound of the Rushing River.

"We're almost there!" Jessie shouted in Woody's ear.

Bullseye skidded to a stop on the river's bank. Woody and Jessie jumped down and surveyed the situation. They spotted the calf right away. He was wedged against a rock in the middle of the current, struggling and mooing frantically. His tail splashed and his legs thrashed as he tried to free himself from the rock.

"There he is!" Jessie exclaimed. "He's stuck now, but it looks like he's trying to get loose. If

he does, he might be swept downriver!"

Woody nodded, looking worried. "Now what do we do? We have to get him out of there! But we need a way to keep the current from pulling him away!"

"I know what we can do." Jessie grabbed her lasso. Racing to the edge of the river, she paused to aim.

She gulped. It was a long way out to the middle of the river, where the calf was stuck. Could she do it?

All she could do was try her best. She let the lasso fly. The rope snaked out, out, out across the rumbling, tumbling water . . . and landed neatly around the calf's neck.

"Moooooo!" the calf bellowed.

"Yee-hah!" Jessie cried. "I got it!"

"Good job!" Woody exclaimed, patting her on the back. "Let's see if we can pull him out of there."

The two of them tugged on the rope. But all that did was make the calf thrash around even more. He was afraid! Instead of letting them pull him to safety, he planted his feet and wouldn't budge.

Jessie gulped. "Oh, no!" she said. "He's too scared to listen to us. How are we going to get him to come out?"

"One of us will have to go out there and calm him down first." Woody pointed to a few rocks in the river. "Maybe I can hop across on those and lead him out."

Jessie gulped. "Are you sure? They look pretty wet and slippery."

"What other choice is there?" Woody said bravely. "I'll be okay. Don't worry."

"I'll hold on to the rope," Jessie said. "When you get to the calf, Bullseye and I will help pull."

Woody nodded and took a deep breath. He was trying to be brave, but Jessie was right. The rocks looked pretty scary.

"Here I go," he said. He stepped off the bank onto the closest rock. It felt slippery beneath his boots, but he tried not to think about that. Instead, he hopped onto the next stepping-stone. Then the next one. On the fourth rock, his boot heel slipped on the slick surface.

"Woody!" Jessie cried from the shore. "Be careful!"

Bullseye let out a loud, worried neigh. The calf mooed again, sounding more scared than ever.

Woody couldn't answer any of them. He was

too busy waving his arms like a windmill, trying to keep from pitching face-forward into the fast-moving, frothy water.

After a few seconds, he regained his balance. He hopped to the next rock. "I'm okay!" he called to Jessie and Bullseye. "Almost there!"

Not daring to look down at the racing current just inches from his boot tips, he continued on his way. Another rock. And another.

"I'm coming, little calf," he called as calmly as he could. "Don't worry, you'll be safe soon."

The calf mooed again. This time he sounded a little less frightened.

Soon Woody hopped onto the last rock. He reached out to pat the calf on the shoulder. "Come on, fella," he wheedled. "Let's swim on back to shore now, okay?"

The calf seemed dubious at first. But Woody finally convinced him to push off from the big boulder and strike out for dry land. Woody hopped back across on the rocks, encouraging the swimming calf all the way. Back on the bank, Jessie and Bullseye kept a tight hold on the rope, stopping the strong current from sweeping the calf away downstream.

"You're almost here!" Jessie cried excitedly. "Come on, little calf!"

"Moo!" The calf gave one last burst of energy. Swimming as hard as he could, he finally burst out on shore. "Moooooo!"

A second later Woody hopped onto the bank himself. "You did it!" Jessie exclaimed, throwing her arms around him. "You saved the calf!"

"*We* saved the calf," Woody corrected her, pushing his hat back and wiping his forehead. He smiled at Jessie. "Both of us."

55

8. The Best in the West!

"What happened?" the Prospector wheezed, kicking his heels to keep Ol' Diablo plodding toward them. The old bull sighed loudly, took a few more steps, then collapsed on the ground, yawning widely. The Prospector tumbled off his back and brushed himself off. "Well? Let's hear it. What did I miss?"

"Woody saved the day," Jessie declared, hugging the wet calf. "He's the greatest and the bravest cowpoke ever."

"Huh?" the Prospector said looking surprised. "What do you mean, Jessie?"

"He rescued the calf," Jessie explained. "He danced right out on those wet rocks as if they were a smooth dance floor and grabbed the calf."

"True," Woody agreed. "But Jessie is the real hero."

"Say what?" the Prospector looked even more surprised. "Come again, Sheriff?"

"She was the one who really saved the calf," Woody went on proudly. "If Jessie hadn't lassoed the calf like the incredible cowpoke she is, he might have washed away down the river before I could get to him."

"Well, maybe that's true," Jessie admitted

modestly. "But I never could have saved the calf without you, Woody."

Woody shrugged. "And I never could have saved the calf without you, Jessie."

The Prospector threw up his hands. "But this is terrible!" he cried.

"What do you mean?" Jessie asked.

The Prospector shook his head sadly. "I mean we're no closer to having a winner of this dad-burn contest," he said. "We *still* don't know which one of you is the roughest, toughest, all-time awesomest, gosh-darn greatest cowpoke in this town!"

"Sure we do," Jessie said.

The Prospector blinked. "We do?"

Woody nodded. "Uh-huh," he said. "We do."

He grinned at Jessie. Jessie grinned back at him. Then they both turned and grinned at the Prospector.

The Prospector crossed his arms. "Well?" he snapped. "Are you going to keep me guessing till *all* the cows come home, you weaselly whipper-snappers? Or are you going to give me an answer?"

"The answer is, we're *both* great cowpokes," Jessie explained, smiling at Woody.

"That's right," Woody agreed, giving Jessie a playful nudge. "And when you put us together as a team, we really are the roughest, toughest, all-time awesomest, gosh-darn greatest team the West has ever seen!"

WOODY'S ROUNDUP

Pirates

AND Horse Thieves

AND Ghosts OH MY!

Late at night, the Prospector and Bullseye hear strange noises coming from Dry Gulch. What could it be? Woody and Jessie join them and the whole Roundup gang tries to solve this spooky mystery. Boy, are they in for a big surprise!

What's going on in this town?

Find out in Woody's Roundup #2:

Giddy-Up Ghost Town

SEPTEMBER 2000

Your favorite characters are back in this all new rootin' tootin' highfalutin' paperback series.

HOWDY Pardners

Join Sheriff Woody, Jessie, Bullseye, and the Prospector as they stir up a mess of fun in the wild and woolly West.

Woody's Roundup #1:
Showdown at the Okeydokey Corral

Woody's Roundup #2:
Giddy-Up Ghost Town

Woody's Roundup #3:
Ride 'Em Rodeo!

Woody's Roundup #4:
Fool's Gold

These titles are sidewinding
to a corral near you
September 2000

Look for these exciting titles from DISNEY INTERACTIVE

Catch the learning buzz with Disney's Buzz Lightyear Learning Series.